For Gorkij, my lovely inspiration,
and Boxer Books for this opportunity

Cristiano Sorrentino

First American edition published in 2008
by Boxer Books Limited.

Distributed in the United States and Canada by
Sterling Publishing Co., Inc.
387 Park Avenue South, New York, NY 10016-8810

First published in Great Britain in 2008
by Boxer Books Limited.
www.boxerbooks.com

Original idea and illustrations copyright © 2008 Cristiano Sorrentino
Storyline by Teddy Slater

ISBN 10: 1-905417-81-0
ISBN 13: 978-1-905417-81-0

1 3 5 7 9 10 8 6 4 2

Printed in China

I Love Korky

Cristiano Sorrentino

Storyline by Teddy Slater

Boxer Books

Korky is naughty.

Korky is nice.

He never barks once.
He always barks twice.

He has a big ball.

But he'd rather have two.

When it comes to soft toys,
he has more than a few.

Korky loves
to chase butterflies...

Frisbees...

his tail...

and the kindly old mailman
who comes with the mail.

Korky begs for a biscuit,
but prefers a whole bowl.

He can chew through
a shoe—heel, toe, and sole.

Yes, making a mess—that's
what Korky does best!

And still, when all his mischief is done,

there's no other dog who is quite as much fun.

Korky's hug-able...

tug-able...

and ever so snug-able.

He trots by my side
when I go for a walk.

He always listens
when I talk.

Korky kisses my nose
when I feel sad.

He's the best friend
I've ever had.